Love
GoGo

Introduction

So many years had
gone by, days became
endless nightmares,
until the day I heard
her voice, and then
theres was hope, hope
that in this hell I

wasn't alone, her name was GoGo, and in that dark place she was my closest friend. You see my name is Alison, and for more years then I can remember I have been used by men for their pleasure, raped and beaten, day in and day out, my prison, was darkness, my eyes taped shut, only catching glimpses of light every other week after the tape would start peeling off just to be forced back into darkness as fresh tape seals me back into my own head. I got lost in my thoughts to the point I could block out the screams, the cries and sounds of men laughing and enjoying the pain they inflicted on us. I didn't know the other girls but I knew their pain, and it was that pain that linked us, but GoGo was different, she was in the stall right next to mine, she was new, and the moment she spoke to me the small steal porter potty that had been my cage for so long almost fell away, it had been so long since I spoke to anyone, and as much as I was thankful i had her, I knew that the mechanic would tare her soul out as he had done to me and every other girl he kept in his world, a world of stalls chained closed only opened for a girl to be dragged out and used for his and his clients twisted pleasures. years ago I said the mechanic would never break me, I was wrong, I can't remember the day it happened but I gave up on living long ago.

Episode 1

The first day was rough on GoGo, she gasped deeply for air,

gagging from the
thick stench of piss
and shit that filled the
stalls we all were
forced to call home,
but instead of fear in
her voice, it just
seemed like she was
pissed off, I can
remember being so
confused as I listened
to her curse and
scream like a wild
woman, I couldn't
help but think she was

brave and I wished I could be brave like her. Then as calmly as talking to a friend in school she said to me as if she knew I had my ear pressed up against the wall. GoGo; "hey, where the fuck are we"

I was speechless, I hadn't spoke to anyone in years and really didn't even know if i remembered how, before I could even think of what to say, I could hear the chains sealing my stall rattling as the locks were removed, in all the excitement of getting a new roommate I forgot it was cleaning day, once a week the mechanics cleaning crew comes by each stall hosing down the girls, the water burns like liquid fire, theres nowhere to run chained to a small toilet stoping you from even being able to stand, theres nothing you can do but sit there and burn as the water washes over you, over flowing the toilet beneath you creating a muddy sludge that races out the stall towards a

freedom you know
you will never have. I
can remember that
day, GoGo never
screamed as she was
being hosed, not
once, she was dead set
on not giving him and
ounce of satisfaction
in her pain, but I
knew how she felt, the
shock of the heat and
pressure of the water
for the first time is
terrifying, most girls

pass out from the pain, I don't know if GoGo passed out, but I do know it would be hours before I heard her voice again that day. Six clients came that day, over the years I had to teach myself how to discern each one of them from one another seeing as there were eighty seven in total and some were far worse then others. I listened closely to them speak to judge the distance between them and me and GoGo's stalls, counting their footsteps so I could tell which stalls they stopped at and which girls they chose for the day, out of the six, one was horrifying, the name I gave him was "the clock man" I had experienced his form of pleasure to many times to recall, he is who worried me for GoGo, I knew she wasn't ready to be subjected to any of them but "the clock man" would be the worst. Luckily we were both spared that day and it wasn't long after that GoGo spoke to me once again.

GoGo; "hey, whats your name"

I was so scared I would let my chance to speak to her slip away again, so like a nervous reck I screamed

Alison; "Alison"

She laughed so happily, it was like we were just two girls at a sleep over, and in that moment I found myself doing something I hadn't done in years, I was smiling. That day me and GoGo spoke for hours, she wanted to know how I ended up there, it was sort of a strange question at

first because I
couldn't remember
my life before the hell
I was living in, in fact
it was starting to feel
normal, a thought
that terrified me
considering I had seen
what happens to girls
that give in and
except the world the
mechanic created for
us. You see, my story
started out pretty
normal considering, I

had a normal childhood, my parents were great, even though when I was with them I didn't feel that way, a feeling that haunts me now. like most teens I rebelled, at thirteen I decided I was mature enough to make my own decision, so when I met an older guy online I jumped at the opportunity to prove I was no longer a kid, instead I was a grown women. The worst decision of my life was refusing to just be a kid, I now see how stupid I was, and it was that ignorance that led me to a guy named Ethan, whether that was his real name I may never know, however at the time he was perfect, a far cry from the simple minded boys I went to school with. Ethan was everything to me, and for three weeks our online relationship felt like a dream, so much so, we were planning to run away together, I had everything planned out, we would travel the world together, get married and have kids, every girls fantasy, until he asked to meet. At first I was nervous, but I trusted him, so I agreed to meet, a few days later we met up at a local park, he seemed shy at first but I expected that, after all he was twenty four and I knew how much trouble he could get in dating me so when he asked if we could head back to his place so we could have some privacy I agreed. After getting to his place we ordered take out and just talked, he was every bit as perfect as he was online, a few hours passed and I started getting tired, I didn't want to look like some kid with a curfew so I tried to stay awake, but eventually I passed out, and when I awoke, I was chained to a toilet in what looked like a bathroom stall. I told GoGo my whole story, she listened in silence, and when I was done she only had one question.

GoGo; "so how old are you now, if you came here at thirteen?"

It was a question I couldn't answer, so many years, no, not years, theres no way to judge time in the mechanics world, days are based on how long your awake, nights on how long your a sleep, its just that simple. The only thing I could tell her was the truth.

Alison; "I don't know how old I am, or how long I have been here"

It was the saddest realization I could come to, I could feel tears swelling up in my eyes but before I could cry GoGo said.

GoGo; "well, do you have boobs"

With laughter in my voice I replied.

Alison; "what"

GoGo; "well if you have boobs you must have been here a few years unless you had

boobs at thirteen, so
do you?"

I couldn't help but
laugh as tears fell
down my face. she
was completely right I
remember being so
flat chested at
thirteen, the boys in
school would call me
a boy and told me I
was apart of the itty

bitty titty committee, I remember that was mainly the reason I wanted to grow up, I hated boys my own age, but mostly I hated not having boobs. Sadly I got what I always wanted, so I answered her question.

Alison; "yes, I have boobs"

We laughed, but I couldn't help but think, how old was I? I hadn't even noticed how big my boobs got, or how much taller I was and how long my hair was now, so much time had passed, but I knew that survival in the mechanics world meant forgetting the old world, so I gave GoGo the best advice for surviving, I told her

Alison; "forget who you were, hide your pain and your emotions because thinking about a world better then the one we are in will only break your resolve"

She was quiet for a moment, then she said.

GoGo; "fuck that, pain is fuel, an emotions keep us human, and the day we give up on getting out of this fucking hell hole we deserve to die"

Her words were so strong, she truly was brave, but she didn't know anything about what the mechanics world truly was. I didn't want to tell her about the rules of the mechanics world or what goes on because I didn't want to scare her, but I knew after speaking to her that nothing I said could ever scare her, so I

could at least prepare
her. The rules of the
mechanics world are
simple, girls are kept
in there stalls all day
unless the girl is
rented by a client,
other then that she is
fed once a day in her
stall and washed once
a week in her stall, a
chain around a girls
waist is chained to the
stalls toilet, the door
to the stall is chained

and bolted shut, making escape impossible from the stall, leaving only two options for escape, one when a girl is with her client, the other when all the girls are released into the iron maze. At first all girls come to the same conclusion, that they were kidnapped for sex, however, this world isn't that simple, here rape is just a means to torture a girl and it is by far the least painful, but there are rules, each client has his own game, surviving those games is what keeps you alive, girls who lose a game are killed. each game a girl starts off with one hundred pleasure points, every session with a client is one hour long and is timed, even though each game is different the overall way they work is the same, a girls goal is to survive the session, to do so she must have more pleasure points then the client when the timer rings, for each mistake a girl makes during a game she loses points and the client gains those

points, both the girl
and the client can sell
their points for a
pleasures, once a
point is used its
removed from play,
and neither the client
or girl gets the point
once its used, also
both the client and
the girl can spend
points to take away
something the other
has bought. the girl
can sell hers for food,

real food not the slop
that we are fed in our
stalls, we can buy
clothes and almost
anything we can think
of, anything except
our freedom, as for
the client he can't lay
a hand on a girl unless
he spends pleasure
points but he starts
the game with zero
and can't earn them
unless the girls makes
mistakes in the game,

mistakes are judged
by failing to complete
task within the game
or by refusing to play.
some girls were
ignorant of how
important points
actually were, a
mistake that cost most
their lives, you see it
only takes one point
for a client to gain the
right to torture a girl
in any way he
chooses, however

once the timer rings if
the girl has more
points she gets to live,
some girls foolishly
spent there points and
allowed the game to
end with there client
having more points
then them, in that
event the timer
restarts, this is called
the killing hour, there
are no points and
there is only one rule,
at the end of the hour

the girl must be dead.
some girls choose to
take their deaths into
their own hands by
spending all there
points before the
game starts, with no
points to be lost
during the game, the
game ends and the
girl is given and hour
of peace, and
everything she
bought, after that the
timer restarts and the

killing hour begins. there are no rules on how many girls a client can rent at one time, which works out for girls who trust each other considering you can give away points and share pleasures, but only if both agree on it. I have won so many games, I have been tortured and watched torture, created alliances with other girls, only to watch them lose games, knowing they would be killed as I head back to my prison stall. this was daily life in the mechanics world, at anytime a client could rent you, it doesn't matter if your tired, sick or injured from a game the day before, the only rule for being rented is a girl can only be rented once a day. The iron maze was a whole different form of torture, a game created by the mechanic himself, you see that was the rule he set for himself, he would feed us, bathe us, and other then that not lay a single hand on us, but each year the surviving girls would be forced

to play his game,
unlike the games of
the other clients, the
mechanics game has
no pleasure points
and no rules, in fact
you don't even have
to play considering
theres no killing hour
for losing, there is
only one objective,
win, and you are set
free. there are two
ways to win within the
iron maze, the first is

simply escape the maze, a task that is anything but simple, mainly because of the other way you can win in the maze, which is to be the last girl left alive when the hour is up. after explaining everything I knew about the mechanics world to GoGo I was nervous about how she would take it or if she would even understand any of it, most girls die before they even understand where they went wrong and thats not what I wanted for GoGo, I wanted to help her in any way I could, the way others had done for me. GoGo seemed to understand the full magnitude of the situation after hearing what I had to tell her,

she asked me in a
quiet, serious whisper.

GoGo; "how many
games have you
played?"

I answered her
question as honestly
as I could, fearing
what her next
question would be I
told her.
Alison; "I lost count
of how many games I

have played, but I remember all eighty seven clients I have played against"

Before she could ask, I knew what her next question would be, I could feel my heart racing, and like a knife being plunged into my chest, her next question felt like certain death, calmly, she asked.

GoGo; "so how many girls have you killed?"

I wanted to lie, I wished I could, and it would somehow become the truth, but I couldn't, I made up my mind long ago, to never forget what I was forced, no, what I chose to do. In a split second I was back to normal, back to the

Alison that knows what it takes to survive in this world, before I felt I could somehow have a friend in this hell, without showing a single emotion, cold as ice, I told her.

Alison; "I killed three hundred and forty eight girls, within the iron maze"

She was quiet, I felt relived knowing that she would never want to be friends with me after knowing what kind of person I was, after all friends just make you weak in this world, but before I could close my heart to GoGo, she said.

GoGo; "well, your alive right? If you didn't kill them they would have killed you, so don't worry about it"

In that moment the walls I created for myself came crashing down, for the first time in a long time I felt I had someone I could trust. There was

so much I wanted to
say, but I couldn't
find the words and
before I could think of
anything to say, she
said.

GoGo; "hey, Alison,
I'm kinda tired so lets
talk tomorrow, oh,
and where gonna get
the fuck out of here
together ok"

I kept replaying what
she said in my head
the whole night, I
couldn't understand
what kind of girl
GoGo was, she was so
relaxed, I couldn't tell
if it was because she
was fearless or
because she was
crazy, but it didn't
matter I made up my
mind to believe in her
the way she believed
in herself. that night I

couldn't sleep, old scars on my soul were reopened, memories of the sins I have committed to survive in this hell came flooding back, but worst of all the idea that once again theres someone I want to protect in a world where the only escape is to let her die or kill her myself. thinking of what would happened

between me and
GoGo terrified me,
and there was so little
time left for thinking,
I could barely
remember the last
iron maze, which was
usually a sign that
once again the iron
maze was nearly upon
us.

the next day I
awoke to the sound of
my stall being opened,

my first thought was GoGo and if she was rented and if so by who, I wanted to call out to her but if she wasn't rented I didn't want to be the one to draw attention to her, so instead I decided to do what I always do which is figure out who my client was for the day and what game I would be playing. that day my client was "the red chef" I had played his game before, a game that required two girls, the moment I realized it was him I felt my heart sink, the idea that I could end up playing his game with GoGo disgusted me. When I was removed from my stall I quickly tried to get a sense of the girl I would be playing with, her scent, the sound of her breathing, anything that could tell me who she was, if she was a girl I knew and played games with in the past or if she was a new girl, and the worst case scenario if she was GoGo. after making it to the game room I still couldn't get a read on the girl, except that she was new. what happened next was what always happens, I won, and she lost, its not like she stood much chance at winning though, the red chefs game isn't meant for new girls, if only she had time to gain more experience maybe she could have put up a fight, but instead I killed her within minutes of the game starting. The second phase of his game is whats truly disgusting and is one of my greatest sins and regrets that I have acquired, seeing as I have won his game to many times to count, and every time I leave feeling like a monster. the rule of the red chefs game consist of one goal, to prepare, serve and eat a full course meal using the flesh of your opponent, its and ingenious loop hole that the worst of clients use to their advantage to pit girls against each other in games, it allows them to inflict pain and even kill girls without ever needing to earn a single point and never having to lay a single hand on a girl unless they wish to do so. the red chef is one of sixty six clients who use this loop hole to their advantage and each one of them has their own way to use this loop hole in their particular game. their called the sixty six demons, the other twenty one clients are called "breakers", the breakers are simple, in most cases they

only work to score
one pleasure point in
order to rape or beat
a girl but no girl ever
ends up dead at their
hands unless she
cashes out all her
pleasure points,
however their name
breakers fits them
perfectly, they break a
girls spirit making her
desperate to win
games at any cost,
and mainly to escape

at any cost, I know
from experience that
after a few sessions
with three or four
breakers a girl can
learn real quick how
important winning is
in this world, and
thats what I do, I win,
over and over, I win
and regret after each
one, but I'm alive and
those who couldn't
win are dead. even
though I knew I

didn't have a choice
in what I had to do to
survive it didn't stop
the guilt, I often times
would try and block
out what I was doing
and try to remember
a world where I didn't
know the foul, rancid
and rotten taste of
human flesh. the red
chef would critique
my meals which only
made it that much
more disgusting he

would tell me how delicious a girl tasted how well she was prepared and plated, and then their was the sound, the sound of him chewing will be stuck in my head forever but what was worst then the sound or the critiquing and even the taste was the smell, the second phase of the red chef's game allowed for the winner to prepare a girl in anyway she saw fit, so girls were given all the tools they would need to cook. the red chef provided seasonings, a fully stocked kitchen and even groceries to create side dishes. even though the first time I ever played the red chef's game I refused to cook or season my opponent

and instead served
and ate her raw the
red chef made me feel
guilty for wasting a
girls life and death by
first taking her life
and then refusing to
celebrate and
appreciate her death
seeing as though her
death was the reason I
was alive. from that
day, the first day
playing the red chef's
game, I decided going

forward that anytime
I played the red chef's
game that I would
honor the girls I killed
by celebrating their
sacrifice so that I may
live and I would do so
by not crying or
wasting their flesh but
by cleaning my plate
and enjoying every
bite, the only
problem, was it wasn't
hard. the second time
I played the red chef's

game is when I
smelled just how
normal, seasoned,
cooked, human flesh
smells, not only did it
not smell all that
different from normal
meat it didn't taste
much different either.
realizing that I felt
nothing for eating
another human being
disgusted me but the
more I played the red
chef's game, things

only got worse. My cooking got better I excepted the criticism and worked harder to prepare my opponents in order to better celebrate the death and sacrifice of the girls but the better I got at cooking them, the more I began to enjoy the smell of their cooking flesh and just the thought of the taste became mouth watering it was in that moment I knew I was a monster and with every meal I shared with the red chef I began to lose myself. This time was different though, I knew I had to stay strong for GoGo so after the hour was up and I was taken back to my stall, even though I didn't feel like talking I was

worried about GoGo
and if she was alright.
I tried whispering to
her but got no
response, I tried to
keep myself from
thinking about what
could be happening to
her, or what could
have already
happened.

To be continued…